Published by Ladybird Books Ltd
A Penguin Company
Penguin Books Ltd, 80 Strand, London WC2R 0RL, UK
Penguin Books Australia Ltd, Camberwell, Victoria, Australia
Penguin Books (NZ) Ltd, Cnr Airbourne and Rosedale Roads, Albany, Auckland, 1310, New Zealand

3 5 7 9 10 8 6 4

© LADYBIRD BOOKS MMV

Printed in Italy

Busy
Building Site

written by Melanie Joyce
illustrated by Sue King

Ladybird

It's a busy day on Busy
Building Site.
There is a special job to do.
Brian and Bruce put scaffolding up,
and Jack looks at the plans.

Dennis climbs on the delivery lorry.
He has got lots of things to unload.

There are pipes in piles and boxes of tiles, there are bricks and bags of cement.

"Everything's ready," says Dennis.
But what are they going to build?

"First we'll dig a hole," says Jack. "A very big one too. There'll be lots of soil to take away, so we'd better get started soon."

With that he jumps in the big yellow digger, and starts it up with a *VROOM!*

When the very big hole is dug,
it's time to fit some pipes.
They are heavy and strong and
very long, and Dennis can't see
where he's going.

"Mind the hosepipe!" shouts
out Bruce.
What do you think happens next?

"Don't worry," smiles Jack,
"You're just a bit wet, that's all.
We'll help you get these pipes
in place, then we'll fix them
all together."
And they do.

Then Brian and Bruce climb up
the ladder.
It's time to build the walls.

They scoop cement with special
trowels, and splodge it on
the bricks.
It's just the trick to make
them stick.
But soon it all runs out.

Dennis turns the mixer on and tips
in a bag of cement.
"You'll need some water in that,"
says Jack.
He turns on the tap.

But nothing happens at all.
Can you see why?

Splutter-whoosh-burst-squirt.
Poor Dennis is wet again.
At least there is lots of water
to mix up sticky cement!

When the walls are nice and dry,
the roof sits on the top.
There is a clatter of hammers and
a turning of spanners, as everyone
gets to work.

There is just the inside to finish off.
Will they get it done on time?

The tiles are fitted.

The doors are in place.

Everything is painted and polished.

"There is one last thing to do,"

says Jack.

But why is he turning that big hosepipe on?

Because they've built a
swimming pool!
And everyone has come to see.
They've got their towels and
swimming costumes.
There are lots of claps and cheers.

It has been a busy day at Busy Building Site.
Everyone takes their boots and hard hats off.
Perhaps they'll go for a swim!